KU-216-778

This Little Tiger book belongs to:

_____

_____

_____

LITTLE TIGER PRESS
1 The Coda Centre, 189 Munster Road, London SW6 6AW
www.littletiger.co.uk

First published in Great Britain 2007
This edition published 2016
This volume copyright © Little Tiger Press 2007
Text copyright © Claire Freedman 2007

A CIP catalogue record for this book is available from the British Library

All rights reserved • ISBN 978-1-84869-599-3

Printed in China • LTP/1800/1723/1016

2 4 6 8 10 9 7 5 3 1

Cover image copyright © Sophy Williams 2007
One Last Game: Illustration copyright © Alison Edgson 2007
Bathtime: Illustration copyright © Hannah Wood 2007
Sleepyhead: Illustration copyright © Stephen Gulbis 2007
Wave to the Moon: Illustration by Dubravka Kolanovic from
Sleep Tight, Little Mouse! copyright © Little Tiger Press 2007
StoryTime: Illustration copyright © Maria Woods 2007
Under the Covers: Illustration copyright © Stephen Gulbis 2007
Lullaby: Illustration copyright © Sophy Williams 2007
Our Favourite Toy: Illustration copyright © Maria Woods 2007
Feeling Dozy: Illustration copyright © Sophy Williams 2007
Six Little Mice: Illustration by Louise Ho copyright © Little Tiger Press 2007
The Stars: Illustration by Dubravka Kolanovic from
Sleep Tight, Little Mouse! copyright © Little Tiger Press 2007
Sweet Dreams: Illustration copyright © Alison Edgson 2007

A Kiss Goodnight

A Collection of Lullabies

written by Claire Freedman

LITTLE TIGER PRESS
London

Tickle my toes and cuddle me tight,
Just one more game, and then it's
"Goodnight!"

Splish! Splash! I love my bath,
I love my bathtime hug.
Wrapped up in my cosy towel,
I feel so warm and snug!

Splish!
Splash!

Snuggly, huggly, small sleepyhead.
Time to carry you upstairs to bed!

Wave to the moon,
Silvery-white.
Count all the stars,
Twinkling so bright.

Starlight and moonlight,
Up overhead,
Sparkling gently,
While we're in bed.

Let's jump into bed
And cuddle up close –
Our story time's such fun.

We point to the pictures
And say all the words.
Let's read another one!

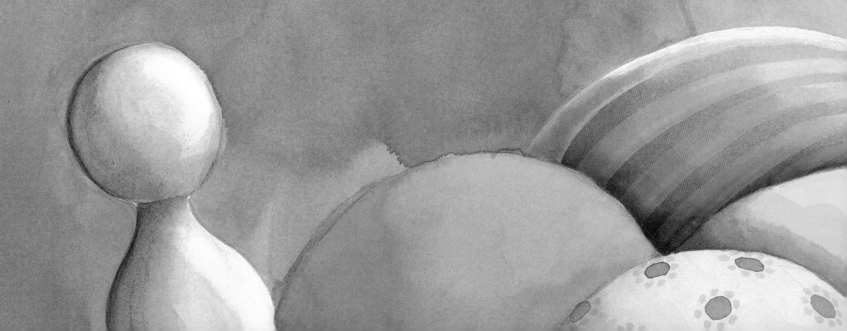

Under the covers, we lie head to head,
Reading by torchlight, huddled in bed.
Just one last story, then turn off the light,
Snuggle together, and whisper "Night-night!"

Hushabye, lullaby, sing you to sleep,

Drift on the music that plays soft and deep.

In the glowing lamplight,
We're tucked up oh-so-snug.
Cuddling with our favourite toy,
We share a goodnight hug!

Feeling dozy,
Sleepy, cosy,
Mummy holds you tight.

Blinking, yawning,
Soon be morning,
Sleep well through the night!

Six little mice
in one big bed,
Curled up head
to sleepy head!

The stars have switched their lights on,
The shimmering moon shines bright.
Just one last kiss before you sleep,
I love you SO, night-night!

Warm in the glow of the lantern's soft beams,
Snuggled together, we're dreaming sweet dreams!

More fabulous books from Little Tiger Press!

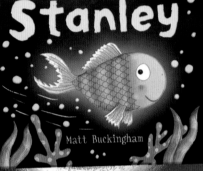

Bright Stanley
Matt Buckingham

Bored Bill
Liz Pichon

Rhino's Great BIG Itch!
Natalie Chivers

OUCH!
Ragnhild Scamell   Michael Terry

THE BIGGEST BADDEST WOLF
Nick Ward

A Little Fairy Magic
Julia Hubery   Alison Edgson

For information regarding any of the above titles or for our catalogue, please contact us:
Little Tiger Press, 1 The Coda Centre, 189 Munster Road, London SW6 6AW
Tel: 020 7385 6333 • E-mail: contact@littletiger.co.uk • www.littletiger.co.uk

Image taken from *Bored Bill* copyright © Liz Pichon 2005